G000155220

Oops, Ow

Written by Michelle Robinson
Illustrated by Connah Brecon

Collins

Two owls.

Small owl.

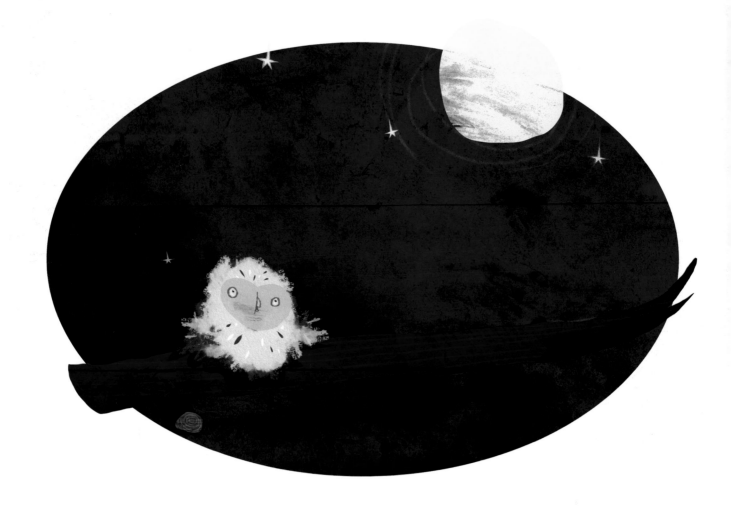

Big owl.

Oops, owl!

Fast owl.

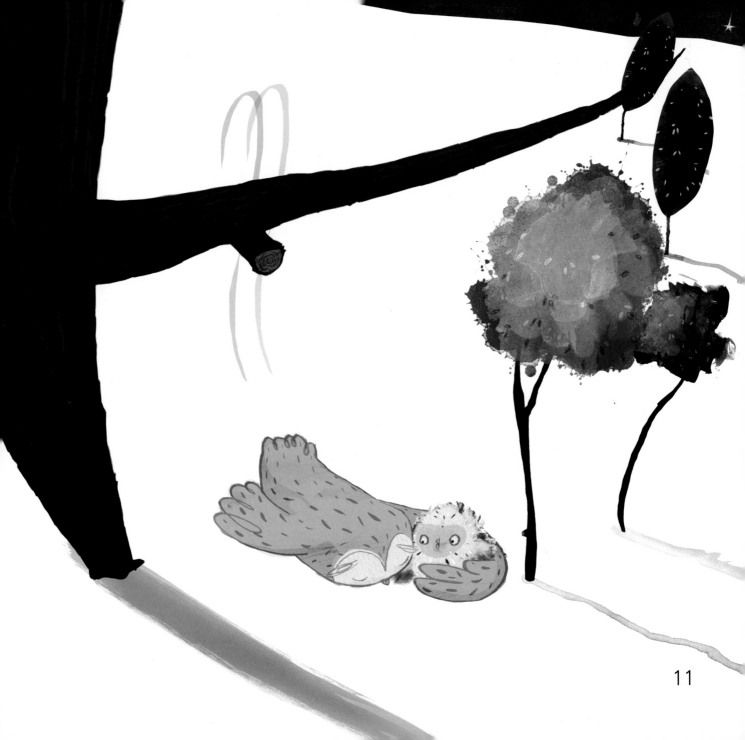

Two owls.

Big owl and small owl

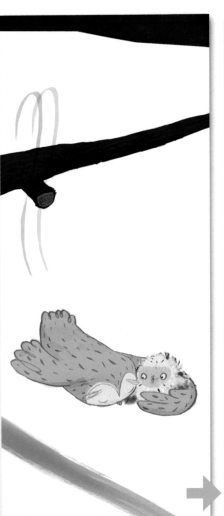

Ideas for reading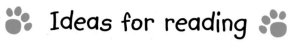

Written by Clare Dowdall, PhD
Lecturer and Primary Literacy Consultant

Learning objectives: children read and understand simple sentences; they demonstrate understanding when talking with others about what they have read; they answer 'how' and 'why' questions in response to stories or events; they make observations of animals and explain why some things occur

Curriculum links: Physical development: Moving and handling; Understanding of the world: The world

High frequency words: two, are, in, the

Interest words: owl, small, big, oops, fast

Resources: picture of an owl or a toy owl

Word count: 12

Getting started

- Look at a picture of an owl or a toy owl. Ask the children to tell the group any facts about owls they know. Discuss where owls live and when they hunt. Use this discussion to extend the children's vocabulary.

- Look at the front cover. Ask children to describe what they can see in the picture. Read the title *Oops, Owl!* and ask children what *Oops* means, and share some examples of when we say it, e.g. *Oops, I have tripped over!*

- Read the blurb to the children, pointing at each word as you read. Ask children to read it to a partner.

Reading and responding

- Turn to pp2–3. Read the text to the children. Look at the pictures and ask children to suggest what is happening, e.g. *it is night time; the big owl is trying to sleep; the stars are out; there are shadows.*

- Turn to pp4–5. Ask children to read the text, helping them to read the word *small.* Ask children to tell a partner what is happening in the pictures on pp4–5, e.g. *the baby owl is trying to jump up to be as tall as the big owl.*